Illustrations copyright © 1992 by Emily Bolam

The text has been reprinted from *The Oxford Nursery Rhyme Book*,
assembled by Iona and Peter Opie (1955),
by permission of Oxford University Press.

Library of Congress Cataloging-in-Publication Data

The House that Jack built/illustrated by Emily Bolam.—1st American ed.
p.   cm.
Summary: A cumulative nursery rhyme about the chain of
events that started when Jack built a house.
ISBN 0-525-44972-8
1. Nursery rhymes.   2. Children's poetry.   [1. Nursery rhymes.]
I. Bolam, Emily, ill.
PZ8.3.H79   1992b
398.8—dc20   91-40927   CIP   AC

First published in the United States 1992 by
Dutton Children's Books,
a division of Penguin Books USA Inc.
375 Hudson Street, New York, New York 10014

Originally published in Great Britain 1992 by
Macmillan Children's Books,
a division of Pan Macmillan Children's Books Limited

First American Edition   Printed in Hong Kong
10 9 8 7 6 5 4 3 2 1

The House that Jack Built

ILLUSTRATED BY

Emily Bolam

DUTTON CHILDREN'S BOOKS
NEW YORK

This is the house
that Jack built.

This is the malt
That lay in the house
that Jack built.

This is the rat
That ate the malt
That lay in the house
    that Jack built.

This is the cat
That killed the rat
That ate the malt
That lay in the house
    that Jack built.

This is the dog
That worried the cat
That killed the rat
That ate the malt
That lay in the house
    that Jack built.

This is the cow with
   the crumpled horn,
That tossed the dog
That worried the cat
That killed the rat
That ate the malt
That lay in the house
   that Jack built.

This is the maiden all forlorn,
That milked the cow with
    the crumpled horn,
That tossed the dog
That worried the cat
That killed the rat
That ate the malt
That lay in the house
    that Jack built.

This is the man all tattered and torn,
That kissed the maiden all forlorn,
That milked the cow with the crumpled horn,
That tossed the dog
That worried the cat
That killed the rat
That ate the malt
That lay in the house
   that Jack built.

This is the priest all shaven and shorn,
That married the man all tattered and torn,
That kissed the maiden all forlorn,
That milked the cow with
    the crumpled horn,
That tossed the dog
That worried the cat
That killed the rat
That ate the malt
That lay in the house
    that Jack built.

This is the cock that crowed in the morn,
That waked the priest all shaven and shorn,
That married the man all tattered and torn,
That kissed the maiden all forlorn,
That milked the cow with
    the crumpled horn,
That tossed the dog
That worried the cat
That killed the rat
That ate the malt
That lay in the house
    that Jack built.

This is the farmer sowing his corn,
That kept the cock that crowed in the morn,
That waked the priest all shaven and shorn,
That married the man all tattered and torn,
That kissed the maiden all forlorn,
That milked the cow with
   the crumpled horn,
That tossed the dog
That worried the cat
That killed the rat
That ate the malt
That lay in the house
   that Jack built.

This is the horse and the hound and the horn,
That belonged to the farmer sowing his corn,
That kept the cock that crowed in the morn,
That waked the priest all shaven and shorn,
That married the man all tattered and torn,
That kissed the maiden all forlorn,
That milked the cow with
    the crumpled horn,
That tossed the dog
That worried the cat
That killed the rat
That ate the malt
That lay in the house
    that Jack built.